About the Author

Jonathan is a thirty (something) year old, who was born and raised in the South East of England. He has the absolute privilege of being a primary school teacher and enjoys bringing children's imagination to life. He specialises in working with children on the autistic spectrum and with profound and multiple learning disabilities. He has a love of cinema, reading, illustrating, football and all things paranormal. He currently resides in Bedfordshire with his long suffering wife, human/dinosaur hybrid son and two fearsome dogs.

The Misadventures of Conkity Cackity

Jonathan Gadenne

The Misadventures of Conkity Cackity

www.olympiapublishers.com
OLYMPIA PAPERBACK EDITION

Copyright © Jonathan Gadenne 2020

The right of Jonathan Gadenne to be identified as author of
this work has been asserted in accordance with sections 77 and 78 of the Copyright, Designs and Patents Act 1988.

All Rights Reserved

No reproduction, copy or transmission of this publication may be made without written permission.
No paragraph of this publication may be reproduced, copied or transmitted save with the written permission of the publisher, or in accordance with the provisions of the Copyright Act 1956 (as amended).

Any person who commits any unauthorised act in relation to
this publication may be liable to criminal prosecution and civil claims for damage.

A CIP catalogue record for this title is available from the British Library.

ISBN: 978-1-78830-657-7
First Published in 2020

Olympia Publishers
Tallis House
2 Tallis Street
London
EC4Y 0AB

Printed in Great Britain

Dedication

Papa. Thank you for providing the magic that has always inspired my creativity.

My wife. The other half of me. Thank you for being the beautiful, constant drive, that makes me believe in myself.

Mum and Dad. Thank you for your never-ending support and love.

My son. Thank you for being the inspiration for everything I do. My life began with yours.
This story is for you.

The oldest and strongest emotion of mankind is fear, and the oldest and strongest kind of fear is fear of the unknown.

H.P. Lovecraft

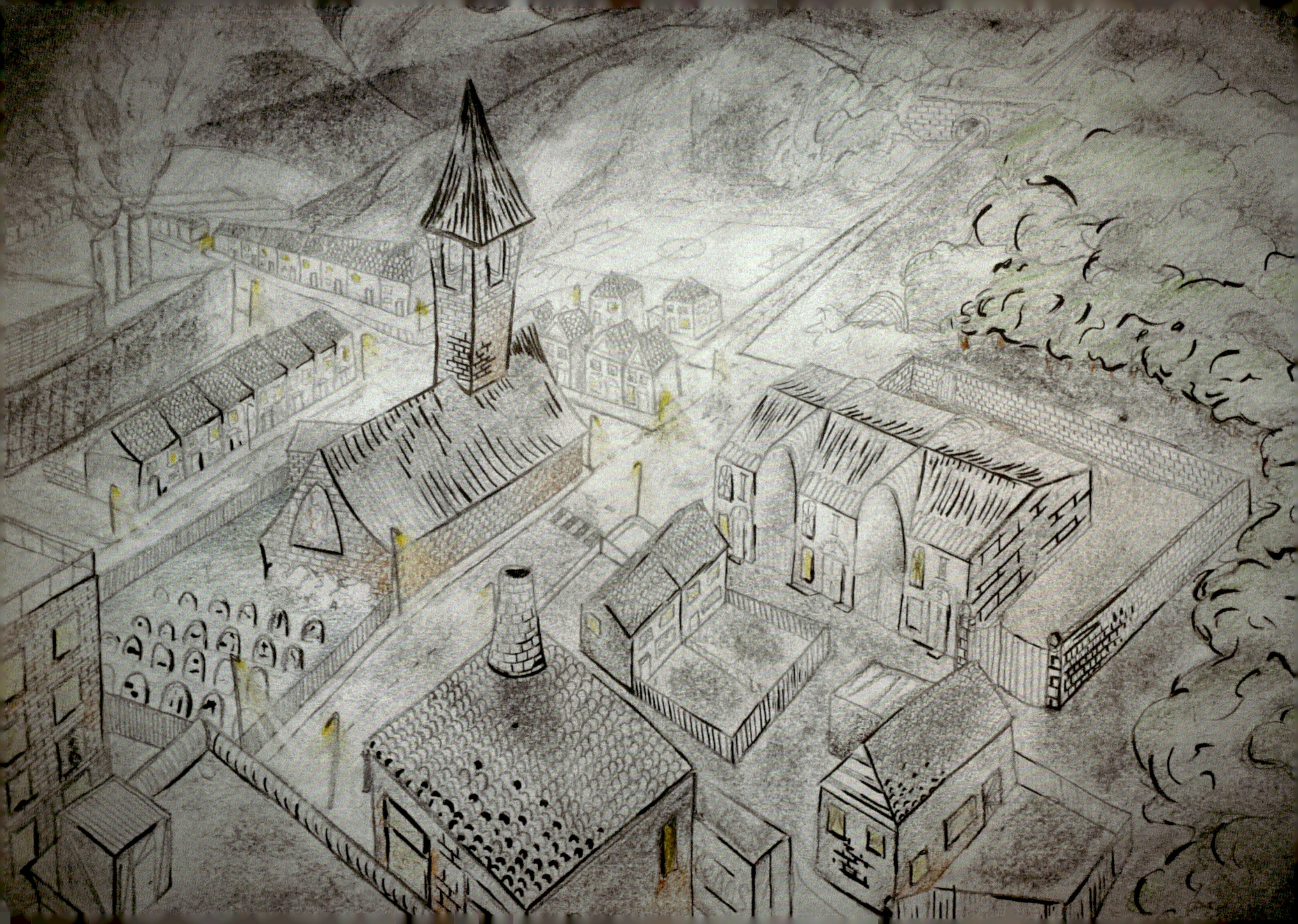

Prologue

Outside of your town, the one where you live,
go down the track by the old railway bridge,
follow the hollow of trees folding over
through thistles and vines and hints of green clover.

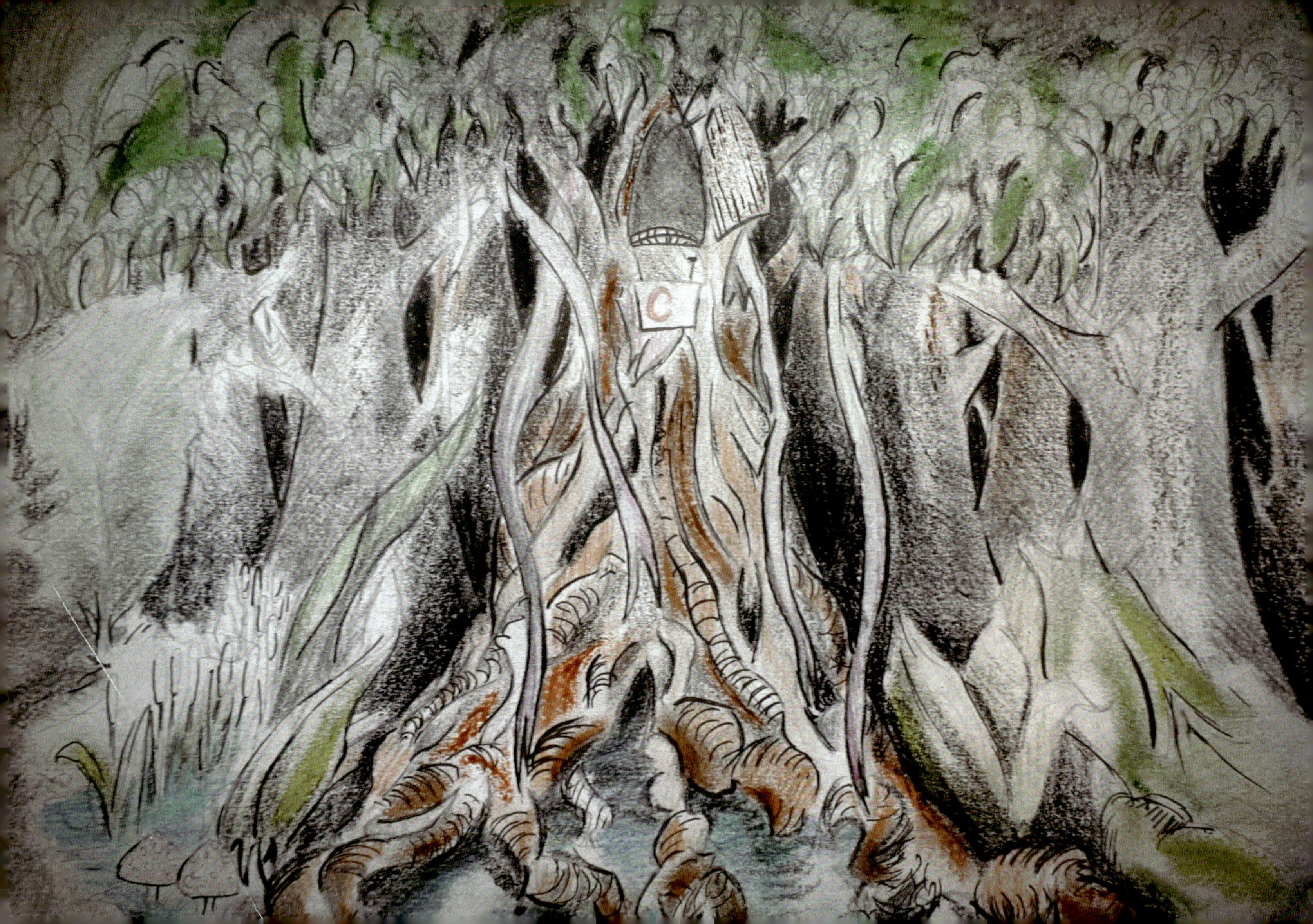
C

Near the mouth of a stream, in an ancient oak tree,
once lived peaceful monsters – a family of three.
Their last name was Cackity; monsters who actually
cared for their precious son, Conkity Cackity.

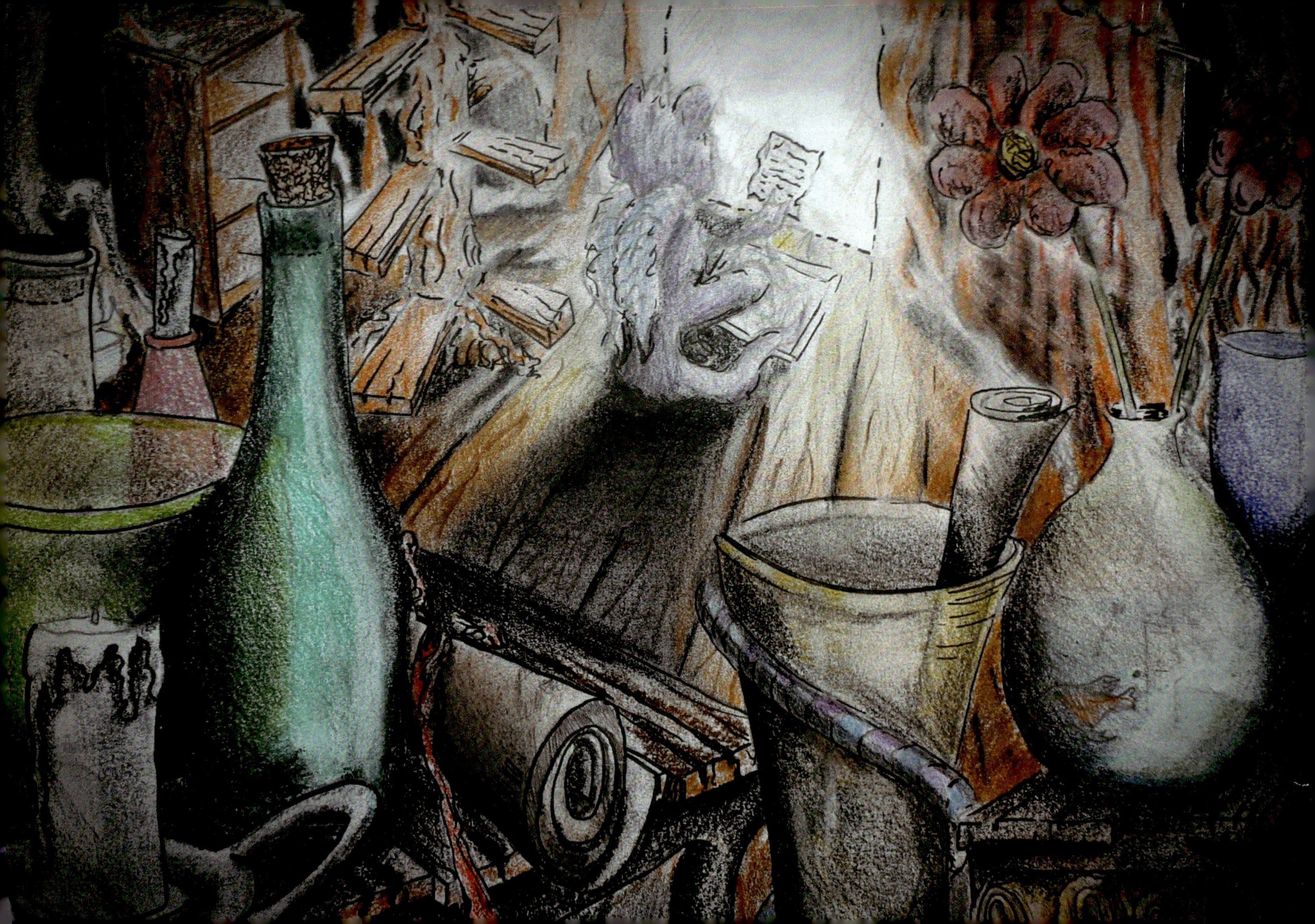

See, monsters in general *(but not in this case)*,
send new-borns to fend and to find their own place
and though peaceful and loving, they're scary to see;
men would fear them and hate them, and not let them be.

£4 To See The Beast

They'd rage them or cage them and not let them go
then charge people money and put them on show.
Cackity's ate just greens or the odd rat and weasel
and kept to themselves, never bothering people.

Never get hungry, their number one rule,
as their kind in the past had been known to be cruel.
They strived to be better and, day after day,
would endeavour to never be a monster cliché.

They would snuggle and cuddle and dance round and sing,
but that's all over now. Let our story begin.

Winter Arrives

The stream had now frozen. Motion caught in a whirl.
The leaves on their home had all started to curl.
Winter would be cruel and extremely cold;
decisions were made for the young by the old.

They wanted to save their little beast man,
quite simple was Mum and Dad Cackity's plan.
Concern for the young monster's safety and health,
meant now was the time he would fend for himself.

And though in conflict with their own inner voice,
this season gave reason and gave them no choice.

Fear

Now Conkity Cackity wasn't so happily leaving forever today!
His mother and father had eaten each other, but left him a note on a tray.
"We're sorry this happened, what else can we say?
Live long, live happy, be strong, not sappy and don't let this ruin your day."

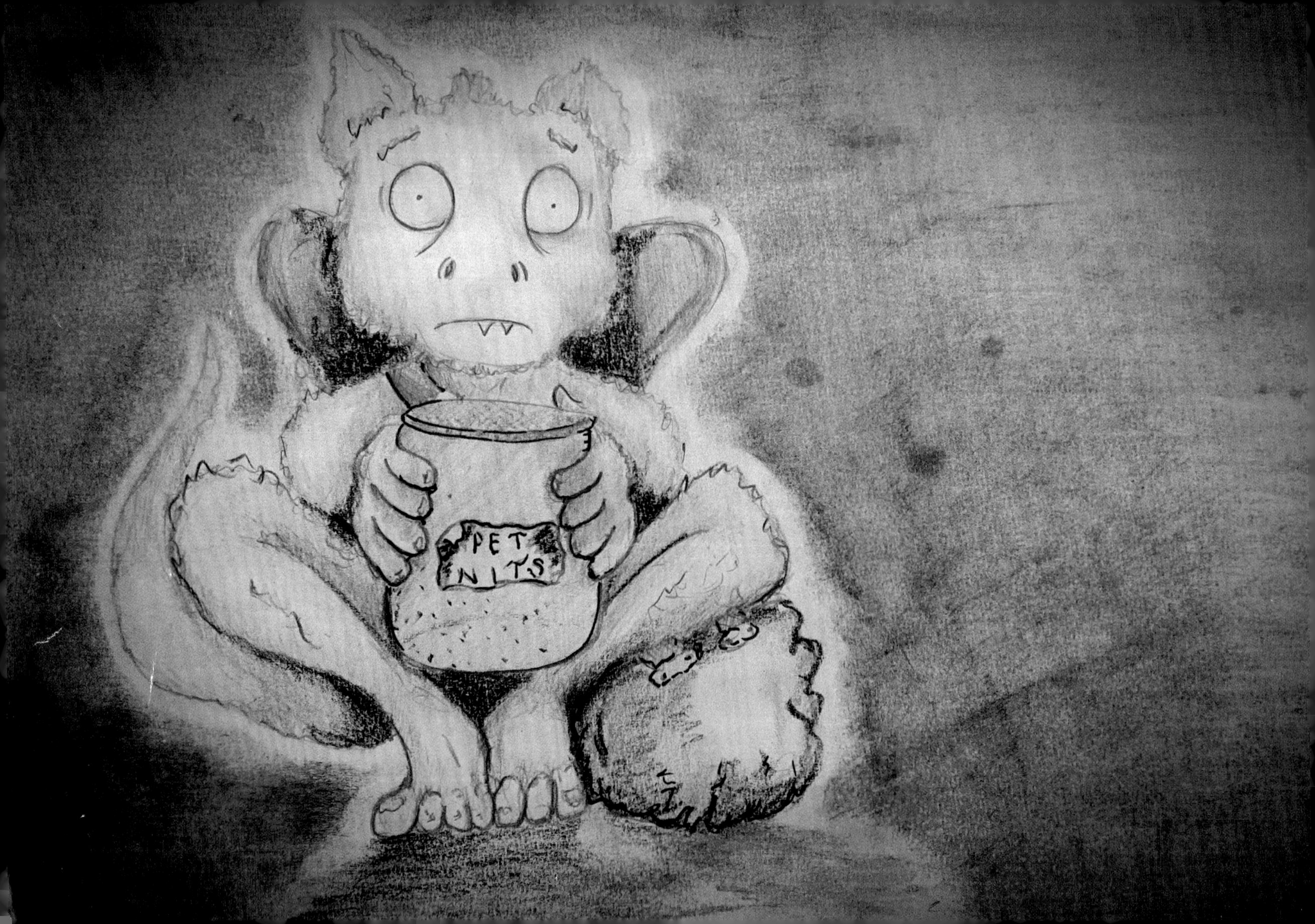
PET NITS

He packed up his bag and feeling quite sad,
swept up the remains of his mum and his dad.
Then grabbed a few bits, some snacks and pet nits
and left the old life that he had!

With an ache in his heart and a tear in his eye,
the little monster started to fly,
but realised quite quickly, this wasn't quite strictly
fit movement to you or to I.

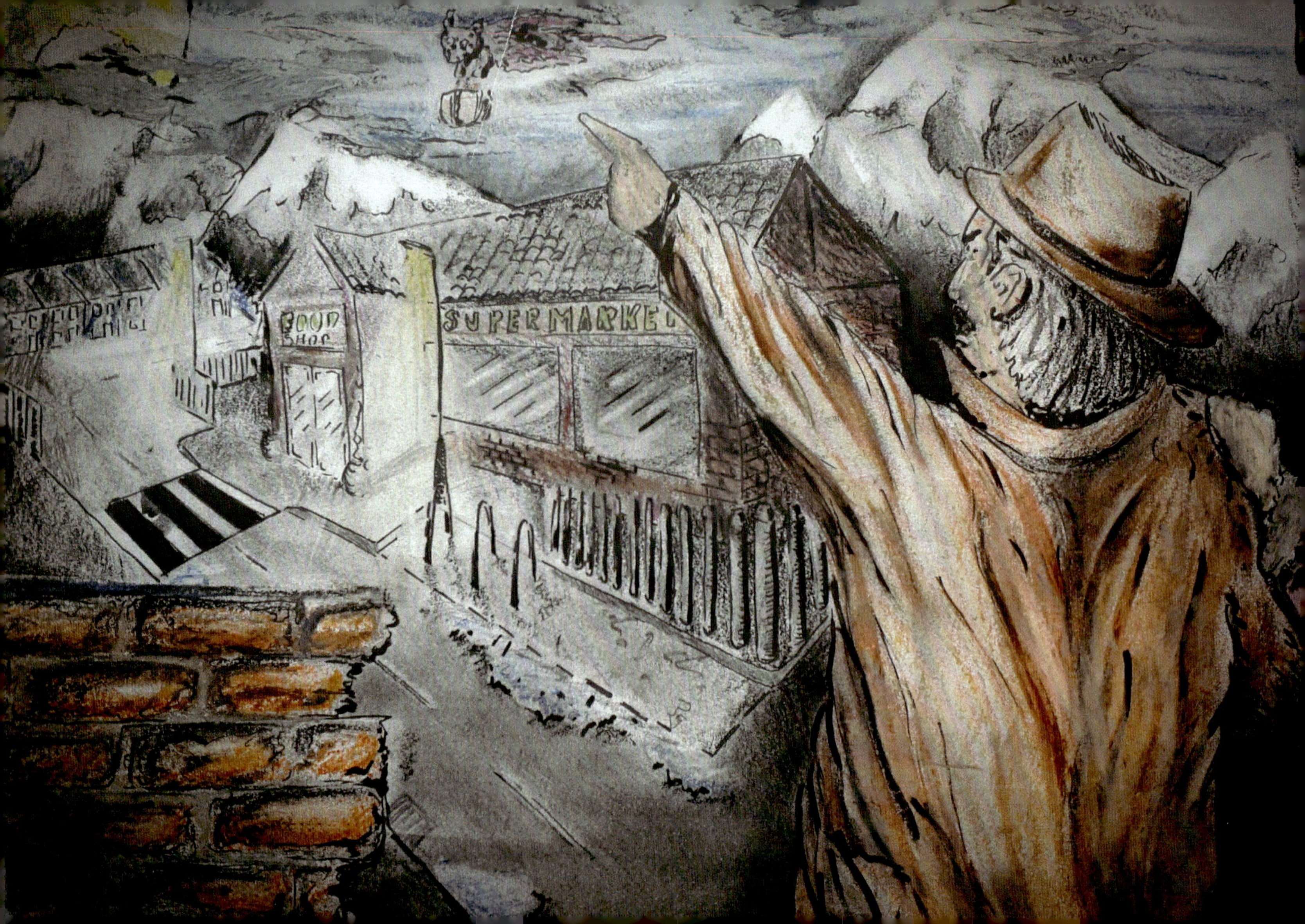
FOOD
SHOP
SUPERMARKE

Humans found him beastly; from head, down to toe.
This soon was apparent, when he heard from below,
"Look up there, it's covered in hair, with has bag and a tear in its eye.
That isn't our normal; it's not what we're used to, so that means this monster must die!"

Conkity Cackity heard these words and now he felt he knew fear.
He wanted to cry, he wanted to hide,
but remembered his parents' note clear.

His dear, loving parents had told of a place
he would not need fear the humankind race,
for he felt that he now had enough on his plate,
with losing his mum and his dad on this date!

"You'll find it up high, away from the eye
of others who don't understand.
Our appearance and language, they can't comprehend
that we too belong in this land.

What they feel is not true; it's all an illusion,
but do not add fear to feed their confusion.
Keep fangs away, be brave and don't sulk
for we know you'd devour a man with one gulp!"

So Conkity flew to the highest known peak,
a tall, snowy mountain, just south of the creek.
When he landed, he placed down his big purple feet,
but he felt slight unease so decided to creep.

He heard a chain rattle,
he smelt an odd smell,
but what lurked in the shadows,
he couldn't quite tell.

One of us.

A hand reached out for him, a mouth leaked a sound
and Conkity gasped as he swung his head round.
Before him he saw five or six just like him,
their veil of darkness now pierced by a grin.

"Hello, newcomer, please know you can rest,
for what's good for you now, well we know that best."

Lonely and sad and more than just scared,
with others just like him, who seemed like they cared.

He placed down his nits, used the floor as a seat,
then realised his bag had started to leak.
Before he could lick up the green residue,
a small monster barked at him, "Oi, who are you?"

"My name's Conkity and I'm now all alone,
but please can I call this dark place my new home?
I've no friends, what's your name? Have you food that you grow?"
Little monster replied, "Wouldn't you like to know."

The monsters conspired, saw Conkity weak,
and whispers, then giggles had started to leak.
Cruel thoughts had been shared, a plan now complete,
"We'll manipulate him to bring us fresh meat."

"Please stay, Conkity, but there's things you must learn.
You'll do things for us for a home in return."
Conkity smiled, he was safe for this night,
but something he felt; well, it didn't feel right.

The Cackity in Conkity

The following nights were filled with the likes
of foods never tasted and fairly odd sights.
Mountains of food, with the odd hat or trainer,
and though feeling muddled, Conk's not a complainer.

These monstrous delights met by huge appetites
were their grotesque endeavours to settle his frights.
When monsters are hungry, monsters grow mean,
so eating's a regular thing on their scene.

But Conkity knew that this food that they ate
gave humans the reason to feel all their hate.
Scraps of clothing some blue and some green;
delicious, yet suspicious, bones were licked clean.

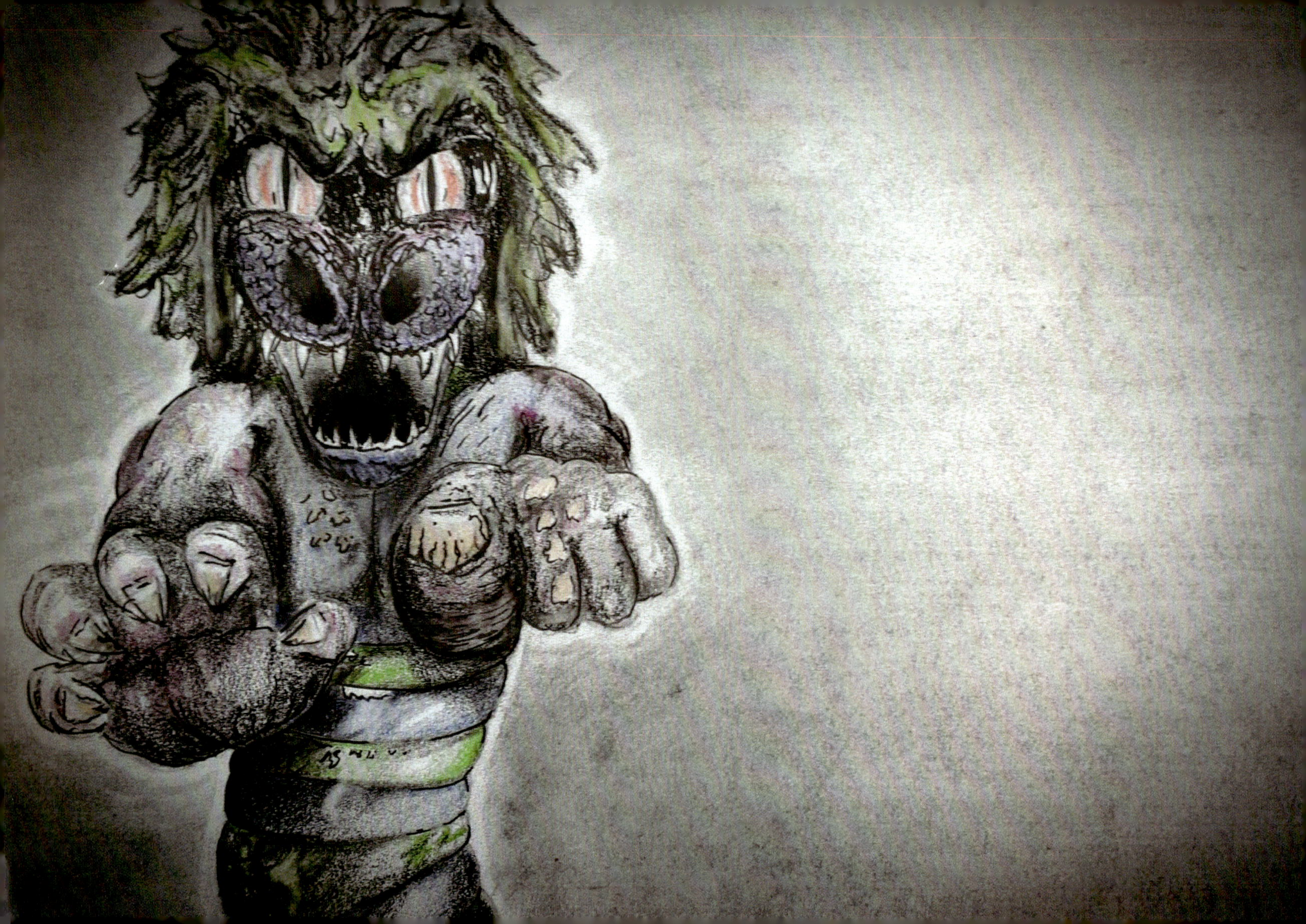

Various metals, gold rings and teeth fillings
shoved into their mouths from stacks up to the ceilings.
Yellow old meat the colour of yolk;
poor Conk came to realise, they're eating town folk.

Since birth, Conkity had always been guided
to only eat food Mother Nature provided.
In emergencies, he'd also been taught,
to always eat food in disguise when it's bought.

Now Conkity knew that he'd lose these new 'friends',
but eating town folk is not right in the end.

Just as he began to make his escape,
the biggest of monsters, with an eyes like a snake,
rose up and bellowed by Conkity's side,
"Here, us man-eating monsters don't hide! We fly down, then grab and take what we want
and its high time, young monster, that YOU learn to hunt!"

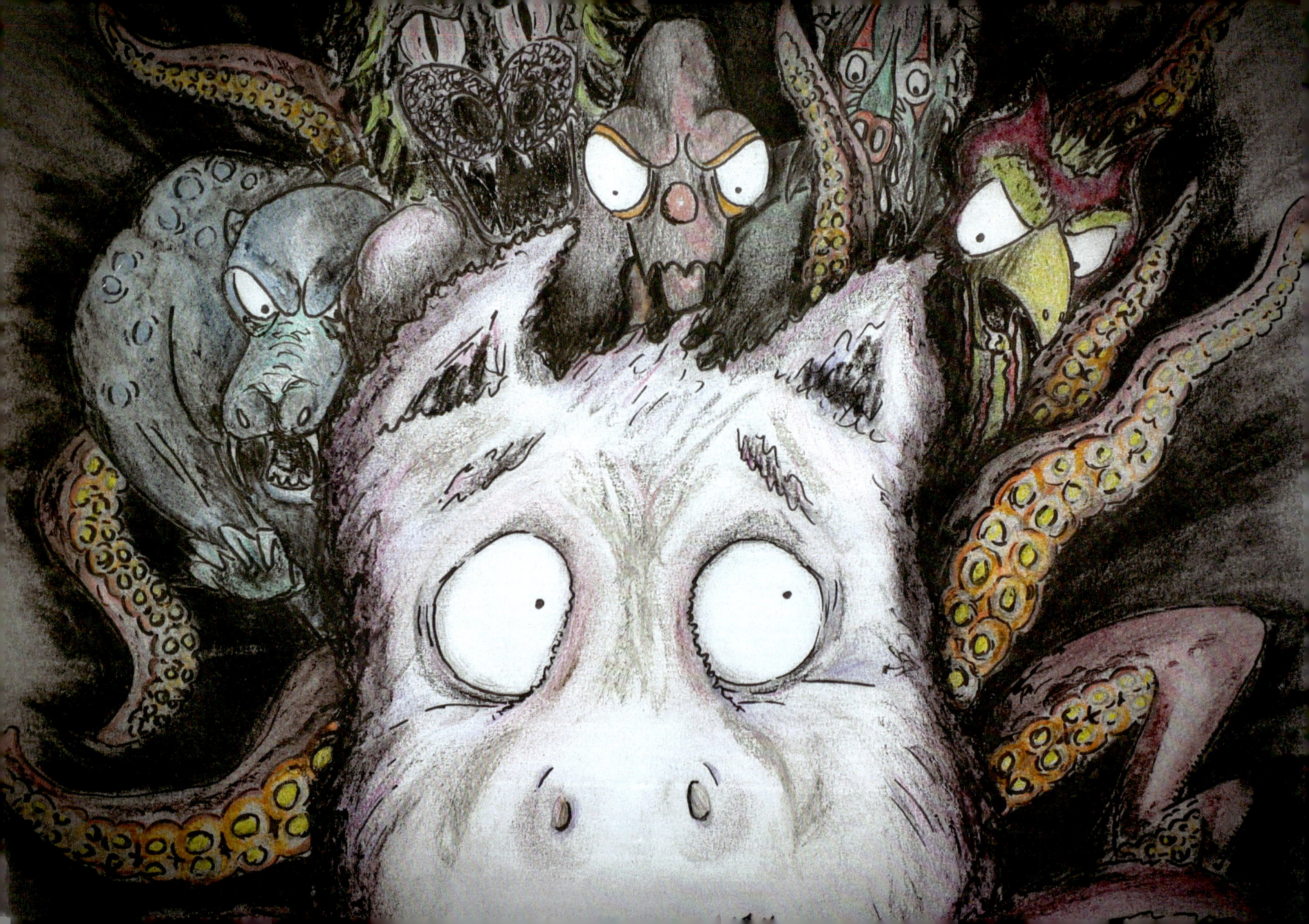

Now monsters should be large, ugly, and frightening,
but Conkity felt the walls around tightening.
He smiled and bowed and said with some glee,
"I'm sorry, but humans are just not for me."

Then leaving his bag but grabbing his nits,
he left for the exit – the others in fits.
He ran out as fast as his big feet could go
and flew through the cave mouth, out onto the snow.

Did they chase? Were they coming? He did not turn to see,
but heard a small voice shout out, "Wait for me!"
The littlest monster, it wanted to come.
"Feel free, you're welcome, as long as you RUN!"

For behind it, a grim mass of monsters did chase,
all snarling and drooling with slime on their face.

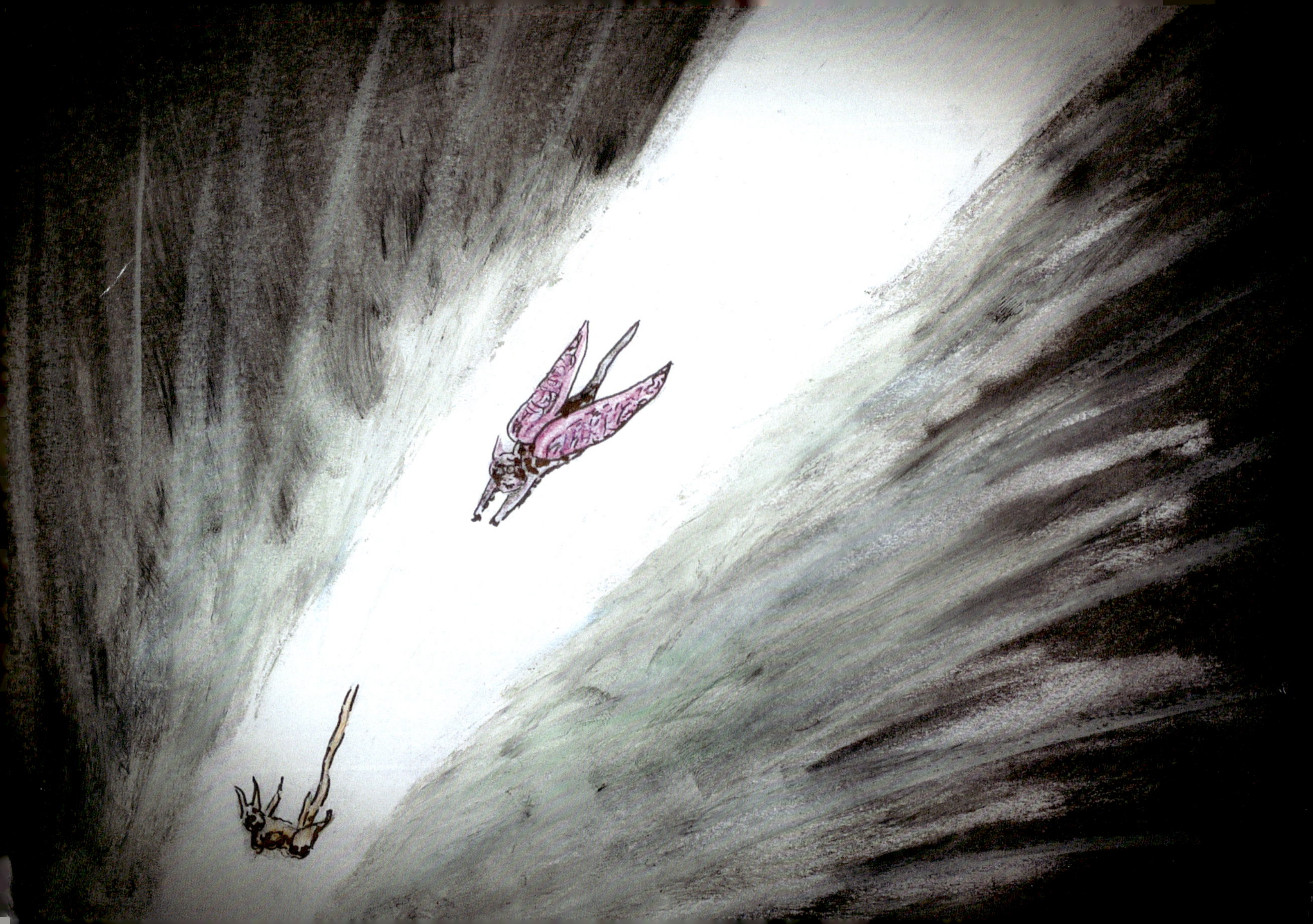

Epiphany

The two reached a cliff and decided to jump,
but this plan had just met its first massive bump.
Small monster, who Conkity presumed could fly,
was now falling fast like a rock through the sky.

A swoop and a soar, then a dive and a catch,
ensured the wee beastie didn't go splat!

Their hands clutched together in friendship, now free.
The little one gratefully said "I'm Bontsy.
I'm sorry before for acting so tough,
but they're mean to me too and I'd just had enough."

Behind, up above where tentacles sailed,
the air turned blue as the monsters all wailed,
"Come back here, you traitor, you're monster by birth;

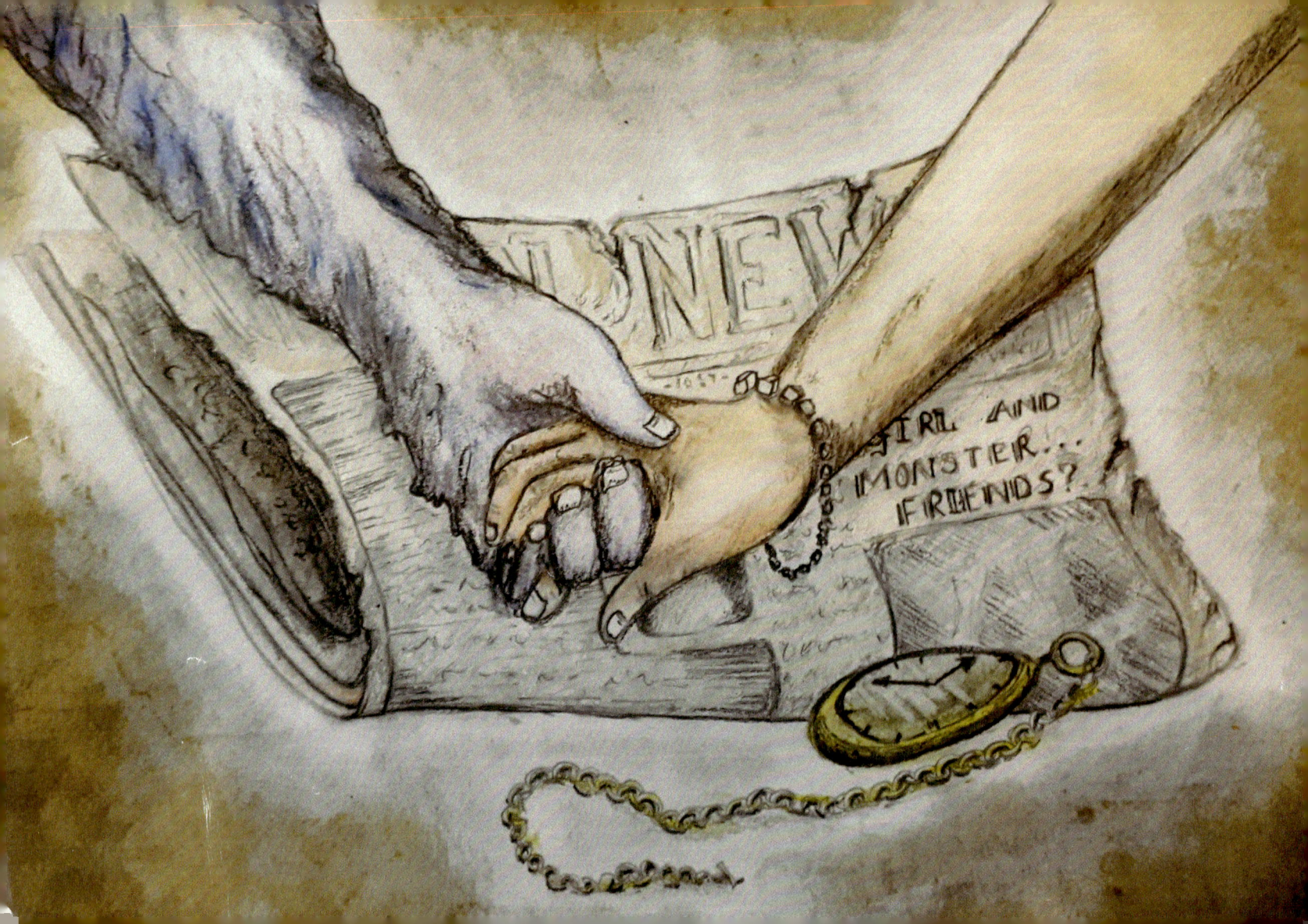

there isn't a human alive on this earth, who'd let you jump off their shiny pitch fork."
Right then, Conk was hit by epiphany thought.
He'd attempt and he'd work and he'd try and he'd do,
to ensure that a human would hold his hand too...

At this point we'll stop, fore our story continues
with a bit of new info I'd just like to bring you.
Remains swept in a cave,
where plans had been had,
were not in fact Conkity's dear mum and dad!

To be continued...